MY MOM THE FROG

MY MOM THE FROG

by Debbie Dadey
Illustrated by Richard A. Williams

A
LITTLE APPLE
PAPERBACK

SCHOLASTIC INC.
New York Toronto London Auckland Sydney

To Cody Uhl for the idea and to my mom,
Rebecca Bailey Gibson, who is definitely
not a frog!

ISBN 0-590-60205-5

Text copyright © 1996 by Debra S. Dadey. Illustrations copyright © 1996 by Scholastic Inc. All rights reserved. Published by Scholastic Inc. APPLE PAPERBACKS and
the APPLE PAPERBACKS logo are registered trademarks of Scholastic Inc.

12 11 10 9 8 7 6 5 4 3 2 1   6 7 8 9/9 0 1/0

Printed in the U.S.A.   40

First Scholastic printing, April 1996

Contents

My Mom the Frog

#1

Aaak!

It all started when I was taking out the trash, which I do every night. I slammed the lid on our garbage can and screamed, "Aaak!"

Mom came running out of the house. "Jason, what's wrong?" she asked. She was panting as if she had just ran a race.

1

"There's a thing on my hand," I shrieked and stuck my hand toward her. "Get it off!"

Mom peered at my hand. She giggled a little. Then she laughed loudly.

"What's so funny?" I asked. "Your eight-year-old son has an enormous lump on his hand and you're laughing." I was plenty mad now. If I'd broken my leg, she'd probably be rolling on the ground laughing herself into a coma.

Mom snorted and then stopped laughing. "Sorry, honey. But that's just an itty-bitty little wart. It's nothing to scream about."

Itty-bitty? Let me tell you this wart was the size of Mongolia. It was big. Not only that, it itched. I think it was growing by the minute. Probably by tomorrow it would be the size of Mars.

"Would you please take it off?" I asked. I'm pretty tough; after all I do take karate. Still, this thing gave me the creeps.

Mom looked like she was ready to laugh again, but she didn't. "I'll get some medicine tomorrow to make it go away."

"Tomorrow? What if someone sees this thing?"

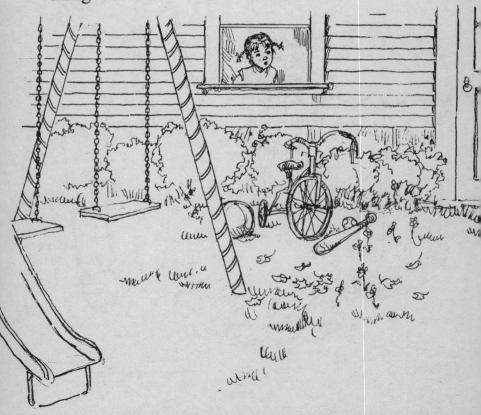

"There's nothing wrong with it," Mom said.

Nothing wrong? My wart made a bulldog look like Miss America. I hoped I wouldn't be one giant wart by morning. "It looks gross," I mumbled. "I won't be able to go out at all."

"Good, clean up your room," Mom suggested. My room! A bulldozer is the only thing that could help my room. Things were getting worse all the time.

Mom must have felt sorry for me because she took my hand and kissed it. "Don't worry. You'll be all right."

How was I to know that my troubles were only beginning?

#2
Eeek!

My wart was bigger the next morning. "Mom!" I yelled as soon as I woke up and saw my hand. "Mom, help!"

Mom didn't come, but my sister Mary did. Mary is one year younger than me and unfortunately one inch taller. Just because she's bigger she thinks she is boss.

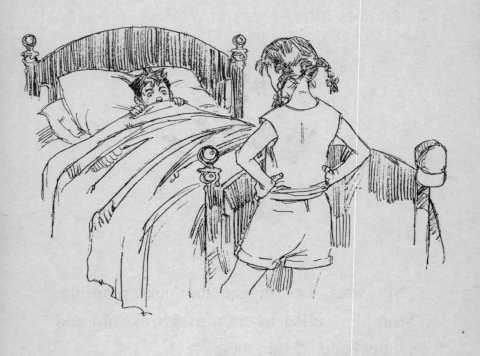

"What's wrong with you? Are you sick?"
Mary asked. I was still in bed with the covers
pulled up to my neck.

"None of your business," I told her.

"Where's Mom?" I asked.

"She's gone," Mary said. "Dad's downstairs eating breakfast." Mary started to leave, then she saw it.

"Eek!" she screamed. "What's that?"

I held my hand toward her. "It's just a wart."

Mary jumped away. "Don't touch me with that or I'll turn into a frog!"

"What are you talking about?" I asked, kicking the covers off my bed.

Mary rolled her eyes. "Don't you know anything?" As usual, Mary didn't give me a chance to answer. "If you touch a wart, you turn into a frog."

I looked at Mary as if she'd just sprouted palm trees out her pigtails. Where did she come up with these crazy ideas?

"That's a bunch of baloney," I told her.

Mary put her hands on her hips. "It's true. I heard it at school. If you don't believe me, kiss your hand. You'll turn into an ugly old bullfrog. It'd be a big improvement." Mary stuck out her tongue and ran from the room.

I started to get out of bed to chase her, but something made me stop. Mom had kissed my hand last night. Mom was gone this morning. I have to admit it made me wonder. It wouldn't hurt to check.

"Mom!" I yelled, jumping out of bed.

Downstairs in the kitchen Dad was sitting at the table, eating a bowl of oatmeal.

"Jason, you want some breakfast?" Dad asked. "Mom's gone somewhere."

I was hungry. Mom was probably just out shopping. I smiled at myself for letting Mary's wild story get to me.

I should know better. I was grabbing a bowl from the dishwasher when I saw it.

It was big and it was green. "Eeek!" I screamed.

#3
scat

"What's wrong, Jason?" my dad asked with a mouthful of oatmeal.

I couldn't say anything. I pointed. There on the floor beside my mother's purse was a huge green frog with black spots.

"How in the world did that get in here?" Dad asked. "Let's get it out of the house

before it makes a mess. Your mom hates messes in the kitchen.''

"Mom?" I whispered.

Dad grabbed the broom and opened the back door. With a swipe of the broom he pushed the frog toward the back door. "Scat, you ornery critter." Mom's car keys clanged as the frog jumped off them. That was really strange. Mom never went anywhere without her purse and car keys.

"Scat!" Dad said again as the frog hopped toward the door.

"Dad, there's something you should know about that frog," I said softly.

"What?" Dad asked.

I gulped and looked at the plump frog. It was panting from all the hopping. "That frog is panting just like Mom."

Dad looked at me. "Jason, don't start telling me another one of your wild tales."

Mary picked that minute to come into the kitchen. "Ew! Look at that fat ugly frog! Is that your girlfriend, Jason?"

I couldn't stand it when Mary teased me. "No," I said to Mary, "it's a handsome prince looking for a beautiful princess. Too bad there aren't any around here."

"That's enough!" Dad said sternly. "It's

Saturday and we need to get some yard work done. Go ahead and start pulling weeds if you don't want breakfast."

"But Dad," I said.

"Don't 'Dad' me," he told me.

I would have argued more, but it was too late. Mom had already hopped out the door.

#4
Frog Mush

By the time I got out the back door Mom was nowhere to be seen. The grass was pretty tall and she could have been anywhere. There was nothing to do but look. I dropped to my knees and started crawling.

"Mom?" I called softly. I didn't want Mary or Dad to hear what I was doing. My neighbor Clyde heard though. Sometimes I think he has supersonic hearing.

"What are you doing?" he asked, squeezing through the bushes into my backyard.

I sat back on my heels and looked at him. Clyde can be a little strange sometimes. I used to think he was a weirdo. After all, his hair sticks straight up, he has buck teeth, and he has a really funny laugh. But most of the time he's pretty nice. Maybe I could trust him. I needed help.

"Promise you won't laugh?" I asked. Clyde nodded.

I took a deep breath and told him. "My mom is a frog."

Clyde laughed his weirdo laugh. "Sometimes when we have chocolate cake for dessert, my mom is a pig." He laughed again.

"Very funny," I said. "I'm serious. There's a chance my mom could be a real frog. She kissed my wart and now she's gone. There's a frog in her place."

"You have a wart?" Clyde asked. "Can I see?"

I could tell Clyde was missing the whole point, but I held my wart up anyway.

"Cool," Clyde said, taking a step closer. I never had thought of a wart as being cool. Clyde's footstep made me think of something though.

"Watch where you're stepping. My mother could be anywhere. I don't want her squashed all over the backyard." The thought made me shiver and start looking again.

Clyde looked at me and nodded. I think he finally understood. He was a true friend.

We crawled all over the backyard looking for my mom the frog. We found nothing, except two toy cars, a bottle cap, and some dead bugs. Clyde kept the cars and I kept the dead bugs in case Mom was hungry.

"This is terrible," I said. "Even if we find Mom, how can I change her back to a human?" Some people might like their mom to be a frog. Not me. I just wanted her back to normal.

"Maybe you could reverse the frogginess," Clyde suggested.

"Huh?" I said.

Clyde fell back on the grass to give his knees a rest. "You know, kiss the frog. Maybe that would change her back."

Kiss a frog? Yuck! Still, I didn't have any better ideas. I shrugged. "Maybe it would work."

"All we have to do is find her," Clyde said.

#5 The Hunt

"Where would you be if you were a frog?" Clyde asked.

I shrugged my shoulders. "I'd be crashed on my little froggy couch watching Z-Force cartoons on TV and eating bugs."

"No, no," Clyde shook his head. "What would you do if you were your mom?"

"Folding clothes?" I suggested. "Mom says she spends most of her time folding clothes."

"I don't think a frog can fold clean underwear," Clyde said.

"No, but a frog could go to a garden," I said, jumping up from the ground. "Mom loves to work in her vegetable garden."

"That's it, let's go," Clyde yelled. We raced back to the garden and looked under every tomato and cucumber leaf.

We found nothing. Well, we did find something, a rotten tomato. "Where could she be?" I whined. I hated to think about spending the rest of my life feeling guilty for turning my mom into a frog. It was beginning to look as if I had no choice.

I figured the least I could do was throw away the rotten tomato. It turned out it was the best thing I could have done because there on top of the trash can was my mom.

"Mom!" I screamed.

"Shh!" Clyde warned. "Do you want to scare her away?"

"Right," I whispered. "We'd better do this carefully. We have to sneak up and grab her. If she hops away, we'll never find her."

We were five steps away. One step, stop.

Two steps, stop. Mom wiggled a little. Three steps, stop.

Now she was watching us. Clyde stood still. I held my breath and took another step. Mom blinked. I was so close I could see her chin wiggling.

Biting my lip, I took the last step and reached for Mom.

Plop! She jumped off the trash can.

"Get her!" I squealed. Clyde did a belly flop and got one of her legs. Mom must have

been too slimy because she slipped out of Clyde's hand and hopped into some bushes.

I dived into the bushes headfirst, but I was too late. Mom was history.

#6
Mary

"What are you doing in the bushes?" a voice asked.

"Ouch," I said, pulling myself out and getting scratched in the process. Mary was standing behind me, shaking her head.

"If you must know," I told her, "I was looking for something."

"What?" Mary asked.

I knew Mary wouldn't leave me alone until I told her the truth. Time was important here because Mom was probably getting away. I figured I could trust her. I was wrong. "Mom turned into a frog and she's in these bushes."

Mary laughed. Her laugh is more annoying than Clyde's. "Where did you get a crazy idea like that?"

"From you," I shouted. "You're the one who told me that warts turn people into frogs."

Mary started to giggle again, but Clyde shushed her. "Don't anybody move, there's the frog." Clyde pointed to Mary's feet. Mom was sitting right between Mary's white sneakers.

Mary stooped down and picked up Mom. "You can't seriously think this green thing is really Mom."

I just stared at Mary. She picked up Mom as easy as spitting. I always thought Mom liked her better than me, and now I was positive.

36

"She *is* Mom," I said seriously, "and the only way to turn her back to normal is to kiss her."

Mary laughed. But then she held Mom up in front of her face. "Its eyes *are* dark like Mom's."

Clyde and I stared at the frog's face. "Its nose *is* pointed like Mom's," I whispered.

"I still don't think this frog is Mom," Mary said.

"There's one sure way to find out," Clyde told us.

Mary shivered and asked, "You're really going to kiss this frog?"

"I don't want to, but I have to," I admitted. "Unless . . . unless you want to kiss her."

"No way!" Mary shoved Mom into Clyde's hand.

I looked at Clyde. After all, he was my best friend. Maybe he would kiss the frog. It only took him a second to decide.

Clyde shook his head and stuck the frog out toward me. I guess kissing green skin is asking too much of a best friend. I gulped and looked at the frog's big eyes and pointed nose. There was only one thing left to do and I would have to do it.

I hope Mom appreciated what I was about to do for her. I licked my lips and swallowed. I leaned down close to Mom and puckered.

#7

Stop!

"Stop!" Dad's voice screeched over the backyard.

Mary, Clyde, and I all turned to look at Dad. He was standing beside the trash can with his mouth open. "What are you doing with that frog?" he asked.

"Oh, nothing," I lied. How could I tell him
that his wife was a frog?

But Mary didn't care, she blurted out the
whole story. "Jason thinks this frog is Mom.
He has to kiss her to change her back."

For a minute I thought Dad was going to
smile, but he didn't. He frowned and looked
at Clyde. "Put that frog down and stop all this
foolishness. We have work to do."

Clyde looked at me. I looked at Dad. "But Dad," I started.

"Go ahead, Clyde," Dad said.

Slowly Clyde lowered Mom to the ground. I watched Mom hop into the bushes again.

Mary giggled. I didn't think she would be giggling when she realized Mom was really gone.

I guess it was silly of me to be so mushy, but there was only one thing left to do.

When I was little, Mom used to blow kisses to me when the school bus picked me up. Maybe it would work. I had to try. I blew a kiss as Mom disappeared.

#8

Anything

Mary, Dad, and I started pulling weeds. Clyde went home. His mother called him for lunch. He was lucky, he had a mother that wasn't a frog.

I looked over at Mary and Dad. They had no idea that life as we knew it was over. No more warm cookies at Christmas, no more lipstick kisses at bedtime, and no more embarrassing hugs at school.

I couldn't really blame Dad. He didn't lose Mom on purpose. No, I just blamed myself.

I know I'm pretty tough. Did I tell you I have an orange belt in karate? Still, I have to admit that I was a little upset.

I sighed and whispered to myself, "I'd do anything to have Mom back."

"Anything?" said a voice from behind me.

I jumped and turned around. "Mom!" I shouted and hugged her tight. Blowing the kiss must have worked, she was normal again. "Mom, thank goodness you're back!"

Mom smoothed down her green shirt and laughed. "I wasn't gone that long, Jason."

"It seemed like forever," I told her.

Mary bounced up beside Mom. "Jason thought you had turned into a frog."

"Don't be silly." Mom smiled. "I just hopped to the corner store to get you this." She held up a black bottle that said *Wart Away*.

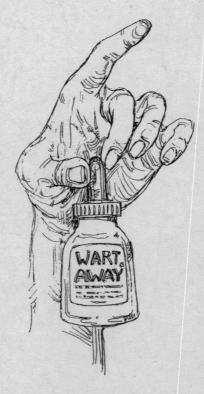

"I wish you had a bottle that said *Jason Away*," Mary teased.

"Let's go inside and put it on," Mom suggested. "This medicine will only sting for a few minutes."

"Sting?" I gulped. "Why don't we just leave my wart alone? I'm getting used to it and I kind of like it. I think I'll name it Herbert."

Mom shook her head. "Very funny, but you're not keeping your wart. Right after I

put on this medicine you can clean your room."

"Mom," I complained.

"Didn't you just say you'd do anything for me?" Mom said. "Let's get moving. I bet the trash needs to be taken out, too." I trailed into the house behind Mom.

This day had hit rock bottom. Cleaning my room ranked right up there with being bit by a rattlesnake. Now, I had no choice. I looked at my wart and sighed. Maybe I should have left my mom a frog.

The Adventures of THE BAILEY SCHOOL KIDS™

Frankenstein Doesn't Plant Petunias, Ghosts Don't Eat Potato Chips, and Aliens Don't Wear Braces ... or do they?

Find out about the creepiest, weirdest, funniest things that happen to The Bailey School Kids!™ Collect and read them all!

❑ BAS47070-1	Aliens Don't Wear Braces	$2.95
❑ BAS48114-2	Cupid Doesn't Flip Hamburgers	$2.99
❑ BAS22638-X	Dracula Doesn't Drink Lemonade	$2.99
❑ BAS22637-1	Elves Don't Wear Hard Hats	$2.99
❑ BAS47071-X	Frankenstein Doesn't Plant Petunias	$2.95
❑ BAS47297-6	Genies Don't Ride Bicycles	$2.95
❑ BAS45854-X	Ghosts Don't Eat Potato Chips	$2.95
❑ BAS48115-0	Gremlins Don't Chew Bubble Gum	$2.99
❑ BAS44822-6	Leprechauns Don't Play Basketball	$2.95
❑ BAS50960-8	Martians Don't Take Temperatures	$2.99
❑ BAS22635-5	Monsters Don't Scuba Dive	$2.99
❑ BAS47298-4	Pirates Don't Wear Pink Sunglasses	$2.95
❑ BAS44477-8	Santa Claus Doesn't Mop Floors	$2.95
❑ BAS48113-4	Skeletons Don't Play Tubas	$2.95
❑ BAS43411-X	Vampires Don't Wear Polka Dots	$2.95
❑ BAS44061-6	Werewolves Don't Go to Summer Camp	$2.95
❑ BAS48112-6	Witches Don't Do Backflips	$2.95
❑ BAS22636-3	Zombies Don't Play Soccer	$2.99

Available wherever you buy books, or use this order form.

Scholastic Inc., P.O. Box 7502, 2931 East McCarty Street, Jefferson City, MO 65102

Please send me the books I have checked above. I am enclosing $_____ (Please add $2.00 to cover shipping and handling.) Send check or money order—no cash or C.O.D.s please.

Name_____

Address_____

City_____ State/Zip_____

Please allow four to six weeks for delivery. Offer good in the U.S. only. Sorry, mail orders are not available to residents of Canada. Prices subject to change.

BSK895